Little Leo

The only true failure in life is not trying at all. Mistakes are practice on your way to success.
To Shaya and Samira. I can't wait to see where your mistakes will take you. —F. E.

ALADDIN | An imprint of Simon & Schuster Children's Publishing Division | 1230 Avenue of the Americas, New York, New York 10020 | First Aladdin hardcover edition September 2020 | Text copyright © 2020 by Farnaz Esnaashari | Illustrations copyright © 2020 by Hedvig Häggman-Sund | All rights reserved, including the right of reproduction in whole or in part in any form. | ALADDIN and related logo are registered trademarks of Simon & Schuster, Inc. | For information about special discounts for bulk purchases, please contact Simon & Schuster Special Sales at 1-866-506-1949 or business@simonandschuster.com. | The Simon & Schuster Speakers Bureau can bring authors to your live event. For more information or to book an event contact the Simon & Schuster Speakers Bureau at 1-866-248-3049 or visit our website at www.simonspeakers.com. | Designed by Karin Paprocki | The illustrations for this book were rendered digitally. The text of this book was set in Archer. | Manufactured in China 0620 SCP | 2 4 6 8 10 9 7 5 3 1 | Library of Congress Control Number 2020931738 | ISBN 978-1-5344-4610-6 (hc) | ISBN 978-1-5344-4611-3 (eBook)

Little Leo

BY **FARNAZ ESNAASHARI**

ILLUSTRATED BY
HEDVIG HÄGGMAN-SUND

aladdin

NEW YORK | LONDON | TORONTO | SYDNEY | NEW DELHI

One day, a little lion cub and his mama were walking along the riverbed.

When they reached the base of a rocky ledge,

Leo said, "Mama, now watch *me* practice my jumps."

Leo puffed up his chest and boasted,

"I can make it in one try!"

"Leo," his mama said, "you might not make it on the very first try."

Leo looked up at the tall ledge. "I can do it. I know I can," he insisted.

1, 2, 3 . . .

Juuuuuu

But Leo missed,
and straight
down he fell.

Angrily, he shook off some leaves.

No fair. I would have made it if there wasn't any wind.

Mama smiled and said, "I didn't feel any wind. Why don't you try again?"

"This time I will make it.

You'll see," Leo announced.

Leo took off as fast as he could.

1, 2, 3 . . . JUUUU

Leo got up slowly, spitting

dirt out of his mouth.

He looked up at his mama.

"Did you see that little bug on the ground? I was just trying not to step on him," Leo said.

I did not see the bug.

Leo walked back to his starting position.

Here we go, Mama. Now, don't look away. You don't want to miss this!

1, 2, 3 . . .

Juuuuuuump!

Leo soared through the air.

He gripped,

slipped,

and

flipped

into

the

mud!

Leo started to cry. "I can't do it, Mama. I'm not strong enough. I'm not fast enough."

As his mama cleaned him off, Leo looked around at the other animals.

1, 2, 3 . . .

Juuuuuump!

And this time . . .

"I made it!" Leo yelled from the top of the ledge. "Mama, did you see me? I made it!"

"Come on, Mama," said Leo. "Now we'll make it . . ."

The Story behind the Story

After everything I had learned creating worlds, characters, and stories in *Shimmer and Shine*, I felt compelled to find a new way to create, and to reach parents and children. As a mother of two, my world revolves around my wonderful kids. When my son, Shaya, was struggling to learn his multiplication tables at school, I put everything aside to help him. We made charts and graphs, and used blocks and flash cards—anything I could find to try to help him learn and grow.

One Saturday, while doing our typical weekend errand run to Target, we got into one of our deep conversations. Walking through the toothpaste aisle, my then-eight-year-old son told me he was giving up on learning. He thought that he would never get it. To hear him give up on himself because something was hard to do broke my heart into a million pieces.

I turned to him and told him that nothing in this world worth doing is ever going to be easy, that failure is just practice on our way to success. We have to fail in order to learn what it takes to succeed. As I spoke to him, a man walked past us, staring and intently listening in on our conversation.

He looked at me in shock, stopped dead in his tracks, and told my son that I was right. My first mama-bear reaction was, *Who is this guy and why is he listening to our conversation?* After we left the store and came home, it hit me: our mother-and-son discussion had touched something inside this stranger and rung true to him.

For the first time, this man's awe made me realize that how my children and I speak to one another is truly a gift. By sharing these "little life lessons," we teach and connect with each other. (And they help my children connect with each other too.)

Maybe, with these stories, we can help other parents and kids talk about issues that may be a little harder for them to have conversations about. Maybe sharing our special gift with others can help them learn and love together.

Through all of life's struggles, every time my kids think they've fallen, I reach my hand out to help them, only to realize they are actually helping me. Thank you to my kids for living, loving, and learning together; for hugging me when I need a hug and helping me even when I don't realize I need help. In your eyes I've learned the true meaning of life and love and resilience.

5